For Gran and Grandpa

First published 1984 by Walker Books Ltd
87 Vauxhall Walk, London SE11 5HJ

This edition published 2001

2 4 6 8 10 9 7 5 3 1

© 1984 Helen Oxenbury

This book has been typeset in Goudy

Printed in Hong Kong

British Library Cataloguing in Publication Data:
a catalogue record for this book
is available from the British Library

ISBN 0-7445-8181-8

Gran and Grandpa

Helen Oxenbury

WALKER BOOKS
AND SUBSIDIARIES
LONDON • BOSTON • SYDNEY

I love visiting my Gran and Grandpa.
I go every week.

'Tell us what you've been doing
all week,' they say.
I tell them everything.
Then sometimes I teach them a new
song I learnt at school. But they
never get the tune quite right.

'Come on, Gran! Let's go and look
at all your things,' I say.
Gran has such interesting drawers
and boxes.

'How are your tomatoes, Grandpa?'
'I've saved you the first ripe one
  to pick,' he says.

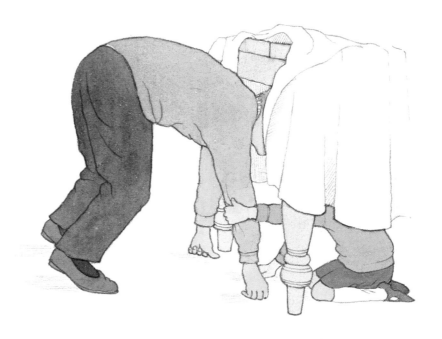

'I'll get the lunch now,' says Gran.
'Come and make a house with me,
Grandpa,' I say.

'Lunch is ready!' calls Gran.
Grandpa can't get up.
'You shouldn't play these games
at your age,' Gran tells him.

'We could play hospitals now,'
I say after lunch.
Gran and Grandpa let me do
anything to them.

'I'll just get more bandages,' I say.
When I get back they're both asleep.
So I watch television quietly
until Dad comes.